The Breeze

Alex Long

Escape Velocity Publishing—Rochester, NY
ISBN: 978-0-692-18678-7
Library of Congress Control Number (Pending)
The Breeze | Alex Long
Available Formats: eBook | Paperback distribution

About the Author

Alex Long emigrated from Europe to the US nine years ago. In his youth he worked as a teacher, soldier, hospital nurse, roadie with Pink Floyd, security guard, made TV shows and movies, etc. Later, as a specialist in Supply Chain Management he became a global traveler who lived and worked in 15 different countries. He speaks six languages and is the author of four books, mostly non-fiction. Married with two children, he currently lives in Sacramento, CA.

Chapter One

I

Top of the World – Dents Du Midi

The Breeze was sitting at his usual place, on the edge of a protruding rock, high above the world on top of the Alps and was lost in his thoughts.

He loved this place. On sunshiny days the light of the setting Sun was reflected on the still surface of the Lake Geneva and from here his gaze wandered around the entire continent, from the Irish shores to the Greek islands. He roamed about these vast regions day and night and never ran out of things to discover. It was like a giant plotting table: he passed under bridges, was propelled forward by friendly windmills, scraped the sky jumping from one tower to the next, sometimes had to dodge those frighteningly fast and loud flying objects Humans used to zigzag across the open skies, he knew every mountain lodge and herd of goats by heart, somersaulted through the missing window panes of cathedrals and curiously followed every parade march, sailboat race or runaway balloon.

Although he didn't understand the languages they spoke which left him puzzled at many things he observed, he was interested to know everything and wanted to get to the bottom of every riddle. But he loved to play most, being insolent at that from time to time. He used to shut the doors in old and windy castles, elevated the balls flying to goals insomuch that they missed them just by a couple of inches and enjoyed the disbelieving cries of sport fans jumping on their feet by the thousand, made the occasional beer-bellied windsurfers wet a few times: he generated riots or surprise and got away laughing.

There were places, though, that he took great care to avoid. Wherever he sensed evil, destruction or misery, he moved on quickly, never looking back. He also stayed away from his own kind when they turned empty- or hot-headed, lunatic or simply disappointed. He considered himself a Philosophical Breeze. He was enticed by enigmas and had a particular interest in the world of Humans. He found landscapes, mountains, valleys and seas lifeless, whereas animal and plant life seemed to be driven by sheer instinct only.

He had to accept, somewhat grudgingly, that he could not understand what Humans were saying, but then neither did his next of kin and friends. To his great surprise he quickly noticed that even Humans do not always understand each other as they were often speaking a different language from one city district or valley to the other. Moreover, even those, who spoke the same language seemed to misalign quite often, this was totally beyond his comprehension. He found the world of Humans amazingly complex and undecipherable. He loved to go to open air cinemas and watch the giant screens illuminated: he thought Humans have beautiful dreams but face much harsher reality.

He even had a few favorite Humans, each of them full of mysteries to him, such as the two he had found last week. He returned to watch them every day, trying to find out what exactly they were doing. He found the Japanese Woman at the edge of a tiny village in Alsace while the Man in the Hat used to sit on the bottom step of the quay by a mighty river.

II

Japanese Garden – Dieue-sur-Meuse

That lock of hair got loose for the third time in a row. The Woman put down the shovel astonished. She didn't remember this happening since she was a child. Every morning she used to put her exuberant black hair up to form a strict bun which never got loose no matter how fierce the wind turned. She glanced at the top of the trees gleaming in the August morning but there was no sign of wind blowing.

The last dew drops of the dawn still glimmered on the bushes of the garden and there was a light mist floating above the lake. Just as beautiful as it used to be back home, she thought in a suddenly overwhelming rush of bitterness.

She arrived at the village on a rainy night three years ago and never left. In the beginning, there was much gossip about her. Nobody knew where she came from, what did she do for a living and what made her run away from where she once belonged. The only one she ever talked to was the shopkeeper lady so the villagers inquired about her at the local convenience store. What they got didn't amount to much, though. She lost her voice along with her son, they thought and finally accepted her presence. She was a quiet, peaceful and reclusive neighbor so they left her alone.

She started to take off her gloves to secure the lock that got loose when she picked up something totally strange. The multi-colored paper pinwheels decorating the edges of the flower beds started to rotate although wind did not pick up at all yet. Then, one of them stopped and started to rotate wildly into the opposite direction. The Woman was raising her hands to wipe her eyes at this miracle when that loose hair lock got into her face, slowly rose and the ends of the individual hairs started to split and curve back until the end of the lock transformed into a pear shape.

The Woman froze and watched in awe as objects around her misbehaved then slowly she started smiling. Suddenly as if she had an audacious idea she dropped her gloves, entered the house and soon enough she re-emerged holding a bottle of opaque fluid and two tiny glasses. She put down the glasses on the garden table, poured a little liquid into them, then sat down, picked up one of the glasses and pushed the other one towards the far end of the table with a slow, accented movement.

– Care for a drink with me? – she asked with a faint smile on her lips.

The Breeze got so surprised that he even forgot about his favorite tricks and the pinwheels silently stopped turning. Now it was his turn to feel astonished. He did not have much experience in that.

–   Er .. er .. me? – he stuttered. In his utter confusion he failed to realize that he understood the words addressed to him. It was as if his friends were talking to him. So many mysteries rendered him speechless.

He witnessed all kinds of human reactions in his life so far from astonishment to outright panic but he has never met any Human who addressed him directly let alone offered him a drink. To his greatest regret, whatever Humans said he never understood.

– Who are you? – asked him the Woman.

– I'm Breeze – he replied.

– What are you doing in my garden?

– I'm .. only playing –, he answered embarrassed as if he was caught red-handed.

– Have you been here before?

– Yes. Several times this week only.

– Why me? – inquired the Woman.

– I do not know – he replied cautiously – I think I like you. I love your hair, your strangely-shaped eyes, your slim figure, your magic garden, your silent serenity. Are you not scared of me? Many others have noticed me before but they were scared, nobody ever talked to me.

– Where I came from – replied the Woman – we believe that everything has a soul, even seemingly inanimate objects, such as mountains, creeks or clouds. Why can't a Breeze have a soul?

– Didn't you take me for a ghost?

– I wasn't sure. Ghosts are more serious and grave, they don't play with my hair and pinwheels. And don't admit when they like me. Not even when that's the case. Do you like my garden? Do you want me to show you around?

– That would be great – replied the Breeze sheepishly.

– All right – said the Woman – come back in the evening. But go now, I have plenty to do. Wait, before you go, drink this up.

The Breeze downed the unknown, curiously strong drink, then lifted up with a single, elegant bow and disappeared amongst the clouds.

The Woman got lost in her thoughts while she collected the glasses. Well, well, she thought, how sad is that? I didn't talk that much with a soul for years. And the one I just talked with is hardly more than a soul. Then she put on her gloves again and returned to her miniature bushes.

III

Quay – Ferencvaros

The Man in the Hat arrived late in the afternoon, after work, with heavy steps as if he walked home from Fate itself. He slowly descended to the bottom of the flight of stairs which was already overshadowed by the mountain at this time of the day and sat on the battered step with the same movement he always had a thousand times before. The head bows, the hand dangles and everything that's been long gone, re-appears.

IV

Valley – Tyrol

The Breeze cut through the clouds, seeking his friends frantically. He immediately had to share with them what happened this morning. In the meantime he was unable to tell whether it was the strange encounter with the Japanese Woman or her strong drink that went to his head.

He didn't see the Zeppelin anywhere, no matter how hard he looked, so he went to see his other friend, the Sunflower, who lived in a deep valley overshadowed by a tall mountain, next to a friendly Oak Tree. So the Breeze headed to this place and turned into the valley at a furious speed. In his free fall he could make out his friend from far.

While he slowed down to normal speed he suddenly remembered that midday hours usually make his friend a bit grumpy. The Sunflower, who was a good-hearted and jolly friend, although from time to time a little narcissistic and touchy, was simply unable to accept the fact that the tall mountain cast its shadow on him during midday hours so he was unable to turn his pretty face to the Sun from dawn to dusk as sunflowers are supposed to do.

The Breeze knew all too well what was coming. In other times he was just smiling in anticipation of his friend's ranting but now he has brought news so important that he had to share them without any further delay.

–   Nice to see you, Breeze – started the Sunflower – can't you move this big heap of dumb rocks to somewhere else? It is casting a shadow on my face, in the best moments, when the Sun would caress my face the most. Oh, how I wish to live on the other side of this mountain! Then I could follow the Sun all day. What kind of sunflower cannot find the Sun at noon?

–   Listen – cut him short the Breeze – you know what happened? I talked to a Human!!! Do you get it, Sunflower, a Human!!!!

The Sunflower went speechless at this. It took some time before be was able to mutter – That's impossible. Are you sure it was a Human? Did too much altitude get to your head?

Nobody ever heard of Breezes, Trees, Flowers, Rivers or Mountains talking to Humans before. These all had their own language that was generally understood and spoken, but Humans? No, the Humans were *different*.

–Of course it was a Human, a Woman, actually. And she spoke to me first. And we could understand each other perfectly!

–   Nonsense – shook his head the Sunflower, in disbelief, – and what were you two talking about?

–   As a matter of fact, not much – admitted the Breeze – but she invited me to return to her garden tonight and we can keep talking. We might even become friends...

The Sunflower immediately felt betrayed. He was very proud of his well-traveled friend and was always happy to see him around. They could talk about the world for hours and hours on end. The Breeze reported everything he saw in his trips whereas the Sunflower was a keen-eyed observer and that made him well-versed in everything that took place in the valley. He often wished he could fly high with his friend but it was enough to look up at the highest peaks above and he got dizzy right away. No, flying was definitely not for his slender figure. He would have been happy to fly over those peaks just once to get to the other side but exotic, far-off destinations such as the ocean did not attract him at all. On the other hand he was deeply interested in the environment, he sensed the changes in climate, weather, winds, air quality and he was aware of the trends.

Humans, with their unpredictable and capricious ways, only meant harm to their friendship. He was just an ordinary Sunflower, although a pretty one at that, he could not compete with Humans. He felt jealousy but was wary to let it show.

–   Well, then, good luck, Breeze, to your new friend. Are you coming back tomorrow to give me an account?

–   Sure, snapped the Breeze, did you see Zepp around here lately?

The Zeppelin was the third cornerstone of their friendship. He was older and more experienced than they were. He was a rather slow-moving, but fast thinking, wise veteran, who – in his time – roamed the skies of even Africa. These days he mostly resorted to Mediterranean locations to bake his rusting parts in the sun. He was a frequent guest in the skies of Andalusia, Provence and Tuscany.

–   He was here last week. If I'm not mistaken, he wanted to fly over to Malta. He promised to return tomorrow.

–   Great – said the Breeze with joy – you both must hear this. Gotta go now, take care, Sunflower – and off he went.

The Sunflower looked after him shaking his head slowly. He had the distinct feeling that significant changes are about to happen and soon. However, he was unable to tell, whether to welcome or fear them. Instead, he looked up and directed his head to face the spot where the Sun was about to emerge from behind that damn peak in a minute.

V

Japanese Garden – Dieue-sur-Meuse

The colored pinwheel stuck into the flower pot suddenly started spinning then stopped at once. The Woman raised her head.

  – Glad you're back – she said quietly.

  – I'm glad to be here – came the reply out of thin air.

  – I wish I could see you – said the Woman – it's hard like this. Can you assume a shape for me at least?

Instead of giving a reply the Breeze slowly pulled the colored veil from the Woman's shoulder, wrapped himself in it and floated silently at eye level.

  – Better? – .

  – Thank you – said the Woman – now follow me. Then she set off on a trail embellished by tiny pebbles and they wandered, visiting flower after flower, pond after pond in the garden that she built with such meticulous care and attention to details during her years of solitude. The Woman showed and explained him everything while the Breeze, still wrapped in the colorful veil, floated in her footsteps without ever uttering as much as a word.

He enjoyed being talked to, the little stories of care shared, and above all he was very pleased to understand all words spoken.

When they finished walking around the garden the Woman sat on a bench tiredly. The Breeze plucked up his courage and said:

– Thank you, your garden is beautiful and it was very kind of you showing me around. Can I ask?

– Yes – replied the Woman.

– Why are those bridges connecting the islands so zigzagged?

The Woman suppressed a smile. Every *gai-jin* (foreigner) asks this question.

– Legend has it – she started to explain – bad spirits can never make it across the bridges built in a zigzag fashion and they drown so we're safe from them when in the islands.

– How can you be so lonely?

The question was so totally unexpected that the Woman would probably have lurched had she not been sitting already. She expected to receive a completely different sort of questions, related to gardening and she was ready to answer them all like an expert. But this one caught her off guard. It took some to regain her composure.

– Is it *that* obvious? – she whispered.

– Where are your loved ones? – pushed on the

Breeze – They didn't make it through the zigzagged bridges, either?

–   Don't be cruel – said the Woman in a shaking voice – I cannot answer that one yet. Not today.

–   I'm sorry – apologized the Breeze as if suddenly realizing his tactless behavior – can I come some other time?

–   If you wish – said the Woman, her stony face revealing no emotions. And they parted.

Next day he didn't find the Woman at home and this made him uneasy. He tossed and turned sleepless on the top of the world, replaying every detail of his visit the day before in his mind, over and over again. Did I go too far? he asked himself. Diplomacy was never one of his top skills, he knew. Also, he was quite concerned about that creepy thing with ghosts and bridges. I'm a Breeze, not a ghost, let alone an evil spirit, he thought to himself, but am I a good or a bad Breeze? Can I make it across the bridges?

On the third day he found the Woman in the far end of the garden. She shielded herself with an umbrella against the drizzle.

– I had to escape from the place where I was born and raised – she started – get away from the man who raised me and - although I wasn't alone getting away - I was finally left alone. And when you have no one to lean on, it's very easy to get confused and no longer be able to tell Right from Wrong.

– I apologize for being inconsiderate – added the Breeze – you see, that's exactly what I've been pondering for a day or so: am I a good Breeze or a bad one? Can I make it across your bridges?

The Woman smiled. The Breeze looked in awe how smiling made her face so much younger as if years would have suddenly vanished. He never saw this mischievous smile before. It looked great on her. She must smile more frequently, he thought.

– Go ahead – she encouraged him – there's only one way to find that out!

– It's not that easy – snapped the Breeze indignantly.

– I know, replied the Woman – it's a terrible thing to live in fear. That's why you have to go for it!

– Let me ask you one thing first – said the Breeze, – the bridges leading to the villagers? Are those zigzagged, too?

– What do you mean?

– If I can make it across, so can you.

Her eyes narrowed. – That's different – she said.

– Why would it be different? For you, it's not a terrible thing to live in fear? Solitude is the worst of all fears. If I find the courage to go for it and I make it, my fear will evaporate. And if I learn to subdue my fears where is it I cannot go to? Same to you.

The Woman offered no reply.

– Well – asked the Breeze, – do we go for it?

The Woman stood up silently, closed her umbrella and returned to the house with small steps. The Breeze dropped the vail in his disappointment and flew off without looking back.

VI

Valley – Tyrol

You blew it – said the Sunflower.

The three friends were sitting in the sun-drenched valley. The Zeppelin contemplated what he heard.

Then he suddenly asked – Do you understand the words of other Humans as well? The Breeze thought about it. Then it dawned on him. How come he didn't realize?

– No – he replied, – just hers.

– Then nothing is lost – proclaimed the Zeppelin firmly. – No quarrel lasts forever, Breeze, don't you forget that.

VII

Japanese Garden – Dieue-sur-Meuse

The Breeze visited the village the next day and the day after but the Woman remained out-of-sight.

When he entered the garden on the third day he still couldn't see her but he had the unmistakable feeling that something changed. He was looking around slowly, inquisitively but was unable to spot it. He was just about to leave when his gaze turned on one of those wooden bridges painted red.

There was a colored pinwheel secured to its handrail. Another one on the opposite site. And all bridges were decorated the same way.

The Breeze was looking at the unusual sight for some time, wondering what it might mean. Then he got it. Before he started moving he took a long last look at the house. He felt he could make out the motionless silhouette behind the curtain. Then he turned around and took off.

He crossed the first bridge a bit hesitantly, the next one was easier and as he proceeded from bridge to bridge and the heap of pinwheels in his hand grew he felt himself ever easier and indestructible, the fear shrank and went away altogether making him wonder what was he afraid of in the first place.

He put down the colored bouquet of pinwheels on the bench with a theatrical gesture and left.

VIII

Dieue-sur-Meuse

The next weekend the puzzled villagers found lotus flowers pinned to the trunks of the trees. When they turned to the shopkeeper lady for clues they learned that the Japanese Woman opens up her garden to anybody interested in the weekend.

A boy with a bicycle was the first to come. He was only looking for his friends, but while at it, he checked out the brightly colored fishes in the ponds. The Woman was happy to tell him about the fishes and taught him the names of the ones he never saw before. When the boy finally got on his bicycle and left, the Woman exhaled as if relieved: she expected all souls in the village to stay away.

But then the boy returned, this time in tandem with his friends and sisters and the parents slowly, sporadically followed their children, knocking hesitantly on the gates left wide open, then finally arrived the fat shopkeeper lady who immediately demanded to know where can one obtain these beautiful plants and gardening objects.

When the afternoon turned to evening the garden was full of other lonely villagers and the Woman could hardly keep up serving them tea.

In the meantime the Breeze was sitting on the back of the Zeppelin merrily and watched the events unfold from between the clouds. When the last of the guests left the garden with a rare plant in her hands, the Breeze slid down on the streamlined side of his friend and they joyfully embraced each other.

Bridges, thought he Breeze jubilantly, bridges. And that night he too had a good sleep at last.

Chapter Two

IX

Japanese Garden – Dieue-sur-Meuse

The Woman sat on a bench on the tiny island, holding a basketful of plants while the Breeze was playfully carving quickly vanishing shapes on the surface of the lake.

\- Thank you – said the Woman, – Without you I would have probably been condemned to eternal solitude.

\- My pleasure – replied the Breeze – I'm always happy to help. Besides, myself, I never felt so, so..

–...useful?

\- Right. It was elevating – he added – and this is quite a compliment from a Breeze, take my word for it. What do you think? Would I be able to help others, too?

The Woman contemplated this for a moment while her hands were busy planting. Then she slowly raised her head to cast a glance at the Breeze still carelessly skating on the lake. Her slanted eyes were smiling.

\- I think there's a way. Now tell me, do you like tea?

\- I never had it – said the Breeze. – Is it good?

–   Excellent. My family has safe-guarded a special recipe for generations. I can make a cup of it, if you wish.

–   Why not? – replied the Breeze.

–   There's a problem, though – went on the Woman – it is complicated to prepare and it takes quite some time. I invited some guests over for the afternoon but if you can come back tonight, you'll have it.

When the Breeze returned to the garden after sunset there were already two cups of tea on the tiny lacquered ebony table.

–   Take this cup – offered the Woman – have a seat, just be comfortable and drink it slowly and carefully as it is hot.

–   You're drinking the same? – asked the Breeze.

–   Oh, no, I'm drinking my own favorite blend today.

Then they both started sipping the hot drink carefully. Not a word broke the tranquility of the ceremony. The Breeze felt a curiously strange, spicy flavor that made him relax eventually.

It was as if he perceived the world in a different way: shades grew longer, the outline of things turned softer and the smells got more intense.

The Woman watched him patiently with a hint of curiosity.

– So then how can I help others? – he brought it up again. – Others have no such magical garden and they may not accept me as open-heartedly as you did. Besides I do not even understand what they're saying.

– Now you do – retorted the Woman. The Breeze got dumbfounded. – The tea that you have just consumed was made using an ancient recipe, carefully guarded and handed down by generations. Whoever gets to drink it will assume magical power.

– What power? – asked the Breeze.

– The power of sleep and dreams – replied the Woman.

– You mean I can make anybody anywhere fall asleep?

– That's right – came the reply – *almost* anybody.

– But how this power can be used to help Humans?

– Well – replied the Woman while collecting the tea cups – you gotta have to figure that out for yourself. Once you know, please, pay me a visit again.

X

Valley – Tyrol

The Breeze spent the next few days exploring his new skill.

His first target was a herd of sheep, grazing peacefully at the edge of a ravine. The Breeze had no idea what he was supposed to do to make them fall asleep. Clueless, he was flying around and above the herd, somersaulting wildly, but nothing happened.

The Sunflower followed the mysterious aerial maneouvres only half-heartedly. He was already accustomed to the breezy nature of his friend. He was just about to close his eyes and turn his pretty face to the Sun again when - to his astonishment - the entire herd of sheep suddenly dropped and turned motionless.

– Got it!! That's it!! I got the hang of it!! – cheered the Breeze.

– What have you done to them?

– Made them fall asleep.

– Ahem – replied the Sunflower, somewhat relieved, as if he was expecting something worse. Still, to be honest, this was spooky enough as is.

– And how long are they going to sleep?

–   I have no clue. Maybe they'll wake up when they slept enough.

And so it happened. The herd spent most of afternoon slumbering then returned to grazing as naturally as if nothing had happened.

The Breeze was frantic about the success of the first attempt. He still had no idea how his new skill could be put to any practical use but it was fun.

His next target was a lone crow that fell asleep in mid-air and nose-dived right into the lake. The Breeze had to summon all his speed and navigation skills to pull the bird out of the water before he would sink.

The Sunflower watched reproachfully as his friend was hanging out the miserable bird upside down on a tree branch to dry.

–   What a lunatic you are – he rebuked the Breeze, who was too embarrassed to say anything.

I have to learn to use my magical power more carefully, he said to himself. You cannot just fall asleep in any situation.

But who has more time than a Breeze? So in the course of the next days and weeks he polished his newly acquired skill to perfection until he could apply it masterfully. During this time he intentionally did not visit the Woman as he wanted to find the answers to his own question himself as instructed.

By now, he could make any living thing fall asleep at will. The time has come to try the magic on a Human. His friends watched his activities reservedly, they knew he would open up about his plans when he sees fit.

The moment came soon. On a peaceful autumn evening, when the slow-moving fog completely engulfed the valley, he summoned his friends and told the story from the beginning to the end. Although, to be honest, he was sure that the end was still to come. His story had a quite mixed reception. The Sunflower thought that it was total nonsense whereas the Zeppelin hummed for a while, getting a sip from time to time from the small bottle he's always been carrying around then he suddenly asked:

– And what now? Who do you want to put to sleep first?

– That's exactly why I told you the story tonight. I need your help. Zeppelin, you are so wise, you've been all over. Sunflower, you have such a keen eye. What's your advice?

The friends seemed to be at a loss for a while then the Sunflower said:

– There's a couple in the neighboring village. They just had their first child born. The little boy is like an angel with his fairy curly hair and playful character but he hardly sleeps at all. His mother can hardly stay awake, I do not think she slept well for weeks now. If you could make the boy fall asleep that would do much good to both of them. Also, the family and neighbourhood could also enjoy a peaceful night at last.

– Bravo – agreed the Zeppelin briefly, addressing the salute to the Sunflower.

And so they did. When night fell, the Zeppelin took the Breeze on its back into the village. The Breeze sneaked through the kitchen window left open and made the little boy fall asleep. The adults gathered in the living room were so worried that they failed to notice the breeze of air but the Sunflower could clearly see from above as the flames of the candle holder set in the window withered several times. But suddenly there was silence and the little boy was slumbering peacefully in his bed. The adults glanced at each other, extinguished the candles and left the room silently. The Breeze got away, too, unnoticed.

The three friends were watching the house in the next few hours holding their breaths to hear if the boy woke up crying but silence was unbroken. Finally they dozed off themselves.

XI

Between the clouds – above the Rhein

Next day the Breeze accompanied the Zeppelin to visit an old acquaintance in Westphaly.

– Dawning on you yet? – asked the Zeppelin suddenly.

– Yep, I think I got it now – replied the Breeze – the ability to sleep is a gift, a way to relax and forget the troubles of the daytime. Sleeping is a blessing. That's how I can help.

– Exactly – went on the Zeppelin – just think about it, how many people can you help by delivering them to sleep. And the ones who cannot sleep, who suffer from insomnia are often in fear. How many cannot sleep for how many reasons? Afraid of tomorrow, afraid of the challenges the future holds, of well-known troubles and unknown threats. Think about it, Breeze. The sick or the elderly left to their own devices or the kids who grow up like weeds on a fence, the refugees forced to flee from the land they once called their own, victims of extremism, hatred or domestic violence or simply the ones trapped in solitude, they all need your magic spell badly.

For the first time in his life the Breeze felt

nauseous. What have I gotten myself into? The thought crossed his mind. My magic power, is it a blessing or a curse? Will I be able to use this magic power vested in me and put it to any good use?

He was still contemplating it when the Zeppelin slowly landed on the left bank of the Rhein.

The Breeze was so deeply lost in his thoughts that he failed to notice the return of the Zeppelin.

–Ready to go? – asked the Zeppelin.

Without a word, the Breeze mounted to the back of his friend and they lifted off silently.

– Who did you visit? – asked the Breeze.

– An old friend of mine – replied the Zeppelin,

– Knows everyone that counts. Actually, he has a few invitations for you, too.

– What invitations?

– the Breeze was flabbergasted. –Word got out, my friend, people are beginning to notice your little magic trick – went on the Zeppelin – and they wonder what else can you do?

– I don't even know myself yet – replied the Breeze, – let alone how could I be of use for anyone with it?

– I believe other people have some ideas on that already, but let them tell you. I advise you to go and talk to them, hear them out – said the Zeppelin. – You might eventually like a few of them.

So that's what the Breeze did. He embarked on a journey the very same day and visited all who invited him.

XII

London, Gherkin

The people he met first wore the exact same clothes, although men and women wore different styles. He was received in a vast, rain-swept, gloomy city on a high floor of a skyscraper shaped as a gherkin. Through the rain he could see from here the river, the bridges, the industrial zones and a few other skyscrapers, some of them unfinished yet, soaring to the sky surrounded by cranes. On other floors he saw lots of people sitting in front of boxes glaring in various colors.

When they complete other similar buildings, thought the Breeze to himself, they will also fill up with people dressed the same way and the ones glued to those boxes all day long. At the street level of the high-risers will appear cafeterias where they eat, laundries where they take their clothes, cafés, bars, hair stylists and the other businesses serving these people. He was wondering what these people here do all day and to what end?

His thoughts were interrupted by a well-dressed man who was apparently held in high esteem by all the others in the room. – Welcome, Breeze, it's a privilege to have you here at last - he started.

– My pleasure – replied the Breeze.

– We had a little brainstorming session here the other day and came up with a few ideas – continued the man, - on how to utilize your great skill in a profitable way. We invited you here today to help you accomplishing just that.

– What does it mean profitable? – asked the Breeze as he never heard that term before. All persons in the room exchanged quick glances, somewhat incredulously. – To be profitable means we make more money than what we invest – explained the well-dressed man in a self-assured way.

– I see – said the Breeze. – And what are you going to do with more money?

– We'll use it to make even more money.

Strange occupation, said the Breeze to himself. He understood the concept of Money ever since he learned the language of Humans. He heard that Money makes the world go round and knew all too well what kind of deeds Humans are capable of doing to acquire it and how many relationships are poisoned by it, with Money being too much or too few or by the hunt for it. Still, he was not entirely sure of Money's worth.

– Who will benefit from the profit you make?

– Our shareholders – came the reply. Once more, the Breeze had to have this explained to him.

– Got it – he confirmed at last. – And how will they use it?

– Any way they please. They can go on vacation around the globe, collect paintings, buy another luxury boat or re-invest it to make even more.

– And all those people I see in this building including yourself, are working to that end? When you will make even more money, your shareholders will be able to buy a third yacht or a fourth one? So they can stake their claim to every little piece of the planet and write 'This is mine' all over it?

– Well, theoretically they can but it's not that simple – interrupted the man – it also enables us to sustain our families, have our children educated properly, look after our parents and go on vacation ourselves spending what's left of it.

The Breeze sighed. He couldn't care less who's going on vacation and when. – But tell me how can I help people? – posed the question finally.

– Please allow us to show you a little presentation we have put together for you to illustrate how can your skill be utilized and how can we mutually benefit from it by leveraging its unique nature. In brief, how can we build a product, even a brand from the gift of sleep. Please, listen attentively.

The Breeze tried his best to follow the diagrams,

trend lines, bucketed lists, target groups, organizational diagrams, and lots of zeroes at the bottom line shown but he soon got lost track and started thinking about the ones the Zepp mentioned, the elderly, the sick, the ones that got hurt. Will they benefit from all this, too?

– Thank you – he said finally, somewhat dispirited. – Can I ask you a question? Does this help the ones who are prisoners? Prisoners of their own fate? Or of their own lack of will? Who can only see the sky through a small window in jail, in the back of a restaurant, washing dishes all day and night, or in a mental institution?

People glanced at each other once more. – Consider our offer, Breeze – said the businessman. – If we combine our resources we can definitely make this world a better place and do away with lots of human suffering. And you'll be richer than you could imagine.

– I'm thinking about it – replied the Breeze, feeling cooped up already, and sneaked out of the building, grasping for some fresh air. He quickly rose above the clouds, took a deep breath and felt happy for the sunshine warming up his face again.

XIII

HMS Queen Elizabeth – Rosyth, Scotland

In the large room, where he was received the next day, everybody was wearing the same clothes again, same color and style, only this time around he saw only men. The Breeze could make out small chevrons on the necks and shoulders. Some wore service caps. There were large, very detailed maps on the walls. This all happened on board of a huge ship the Humans called aircraft carrier. On the deck of it the Breeze could see lots of those frightful machines that he used to see and fear in the skies as they were flying at incredible speed and unbearable rumbling.

– Thank you for coming, Breeze – greeted him one of the men in uniform, who had the most chevrons gleaming on the shoulder, – we heard about your mighty skill. – Thank you – replied the Breeze feeling a bit embarrassed, – it isn't mature enough yet, still have to work on it a lot.

– Nevertheless we find it very promising. What do you think? From how far and with what precision can it be applied?

– I'm sorry? – asked the Breeze.

– Can you make people fall asleep from far

away? More than one at a time?

– Yes, I think I can do it – replied the Breeze.

This made everybody around the table all of a sudden very agitated.

– Would you be able to make a whole army fall asleep?

– Never tried but I think it's doable. Why would I want to do that? This question was met by a stunned silence in the room.

– If we can make the enemy fall asleep without as much as firing a shot then we can win the war – explained the high-ranked official slowly, stressing words one by one as if he talked to a toddler.

– What war? – asked the Breeze.

– All wars – snapped the general, – even the ones which we are only preparing for as we speak.

– Why are you preparing for war? –

– To keep the peace – the general replied.

It's so typical, thought the Breeze to himself, the ones who want to wage wars always preach about peace. Then he left the room without uttering as much as a word.

XIV

Lampedusa

The next meeting took place in a refugee camp on a tiny Italian island.

Here the Breeze could see people in dire need, by the thousand. He felt he was at the right place at last. The people who invited him over were sitting in a large tent and they looked exhausted.

– Welcome at our camp, Breeze – they greeted him, – we heard you wish to help people.

– That's right –replied the Breeze.

– And how exactly do you plan to do that?

– I wish I knew – he said – I was thinking about this a lot. All I can do is to cast a sleep on anyone. I was hoping you can show me into the right direction how this can help. Any good advice is much appreciated.

– Well, we could definitely use that skill, Breeze – said the slender, red-haired woman wearing a stethoscope, who seemed to lead the group – but you must be aware that we are a professional aid organization here. We're helping thousands of people with very hard but well-organized efforts. There's no room here for private actions, all our co-workers must know their duties, the organization, the legal and financial background of our activities, the reporting chain and so forth.

– What does that mean in practical terms? – asked the Breeze.

– We need to teach you all that before you could get started. You need to undergo several months of training, in fact. Only upon completion of the training can you become one of us and start humanitarian work, under the supervision of more experienced colleagues at first, of course.

The Breeze got morose. – And what will happen to those who need the benefit of sleep now and cannot wait months for it? – he asked.

– Well, I do not think they have a choice – said the doctor, lifted the flap of the tent and stepped out into the sunlight.

XV

Valley – Tyrol

And so it went day after day, week after week.

Slowly running out of patience, the Breeze went to all places where he'd been invited to and tried to find answers to his seemingly simple question of how can he help people but failed to find them.

His friends listened to his accounts of these strange encounters patiently.

One day the Breeze arrived in the valley totally defeated. The Sunflower and the Zeppelin looked at each other: his disappointment could be seen a mile off.

– Had enough – lamented the Breeze – I'm done with it. Everybody has an idea as to how utilize my magic powers but their proposals are selfish, greedy and short-sighted. And so many of them are on the wrong track!

– Heartless businessmen, who – under the pretext of helping others, protecting the environment or some other noble cause – simply want to fill their own pockets while appearing magnanimous.

– Politicians, soldiers, policemen and other slaves of the powers that be, who only want to increase their own influence and wealth.

– Mobsters, who don't care about people at all and only want to use the magic power for their own illegal purposes and threaten me if I refuse to go with it.

– Taunters laughing out loud at every argument of mine, trying to ridicule every word I'm saying.

– Skeptics, who assume the worst intentions and always have a counterexample.

– Simple minds, who expect their Provider to solve all issues while they just simply look on and so forth.

– They are not even the worst – interjected the Zeppelin. – They at least take a case seriously no matter how shady or dubious it is.

– The worst are the ones – he went on – who don't care about anybody else, who consider helping others as a waste of time, an effort in vain. Those who hide behind a single pastime, activity or mania. They are happy to pass any amount of time surfing the waves, diving off cliffs, having their nails done or whatever, while they are totally deaf to the complaints of the needy.

– What shall I do now? – asked the Breeze apparently disheartened. – Tell me, my friends, what would you do? When they tell me whoever I put to sleep will wake up to the same misery next morning and nothing's changed? This I know myself. Human suffering and misery are boundless, trying to make it stop is like trying to salt the ocean. Still, still, this is not enough, I can feel it. It cannot be enough!! What am I supposed to do?

– Perhaps seek out the ones who just want to help like yourself – advised him the Sunflower. – To help, here and now, without selfish purposes or hidden agenda. They might be able to show you the way.

– But where can I find them? – asked the Breeze doubtfully.

– I think I know where – joined in the Zeppelin again. – The ones who are willing to help are much greater in numbers than what you'd believe but as they are not so well-organized and loud their voice is often lost.

– Can you take me to them? – asked the Breeze.

Chapter Three

XVI

Salisbury plains

The place where they arrived the next evening was very strange. The Breeze has never seen anything like this before. In the middle of large green plains suddenly appeared a group of huge sculpted rocks that were placed to form a circle. Some of them already fell, lying on the ground. Whatever this creepy place is, thought the Breeze to himself, must be very-very ancient.

– Humans calls is Stonehenge – explained the Zeppelin. – Must be standing here for at least five-thousand years. Nobody knows who built it and what purpose did it serve. It has always been the sacred gathering place of various secret groups and organizations. Including the ones you inquired about yesterday.

As they were losing altitude the Breeze could make out a number of people headed to the center of the circle, shielding their faces from the light drizzle with their hoods. To his astonishment he saw a few other Breezes approaching the holy site.

When he stepped to the center of the circle suddenly all went silent. All eyes were now on him. Soon a tall man, with gray hair and beard stepped out and said in a friendly tone:

– Welcome, Breeze! It is a privilege for us to have you here.

– Who are you? – asked the Breeze.

– We're calling ourselves Guardian Angels – replied the man –, not without a hint of solemnity – he added with a benevolent smile. – In reality, we do not form a society, instead, we're just individuals pursuing the same goal.

– And what would that be? – inquired the Breeze.

– To cut the long story short – explained the man, – we are driven by the intention to help. To fight and mitigate sorrow, suffering and all forms of human misery, here and now, with everything we have to give. To make sure that no soul gets scratched, no injustice remains hidden and no dream is lost unfulfilled.

The Breeze looked around the audience thoughtfully.

– What it takes to become a Guardian Angel? – he asked.

– Anyone sharing our goals can become one. We're ordinary people, bakers, bus drivers, physicians, retirees and so on. Also, we have some extra help – said the man hinting at the Breezes floating outside the circle. – We act quietly and switfly, without any remuneration or advertising our services in any way. You'll never read about Guardian Angels in the papers or news portals, but there's many of them. We are a faceless, secretive but rather nimble and effective force.

– Who do you help? – pressed on the Breeze.

– We primarily help the ones who went down, who have fallen, as it was already mentioned to you by the Zeppelin. The ones who are unable to help themselves any more or yet. But it is very important for you to understand, my friend, that it not only the helpless who need assistance. Everybody can use some help from time to time, perhaps in crucial moments in life, in a sports competition, a piano exam or when they hold their newborn child in their hands for the first time. Everybody needs support, attention and forgiveness. A second chance to start over. The power of mercy.

There was an utter silence. The Breeze was digesting what he heard.

– We've been watching you, too, for some time now, Breeze – said a young woman somewhere in the crowd standing silently. – We're aware of your skills and appreciate your good intentions. If you join us you'll become but one of us, one of the many Guardian Angels. We cannot promise you money, power, influence or wealth. These are useless for a Breeze anyway. If you're a Guardian Angel, the reward for your deeds is in itself.

– But I feel myself so little sometimes – cried out the Breeze – so insignificant!! How could I heal the world all by myself?

– You are not alone, don't you ever forget that – said a voice from behind. – And there's no such thing as a helping act too little or insignificant. If you do anything for the last one of the Humans, you do it for all of them and your sacrifice will not be wasted. You do it for the Mankind in which we're all united.

– But I'm not even human – protested the Breeze.

– Neither are we – said now one of the Breezes floating outside the circle. – Maybe that's exactly why we help Humans. Because we *can*. And that's how we can become larger than ourselves.

– I like what I heard here today – summed it up the Breeze finally. – But before making the decision there's someone else I have to ask about it.

Thus the secret meeting ended and a half an hour later the rising Moon shed his light only on rocks forming an empty circle.

XVII

Another valley – Tyrol

The Sunflower woke up to a world that changed around him somehow. Still a bit dizzy, he was trying to read his impressions but didn't understand why everything seemed so *different*.

Then he got frozen. The Oak Tree!!! It was gone!!! And the valley, it didn't look the same, either.

– Where am I? Is this a dream? – whispered to himself, while his leaves and petals were trembling. He turned around and suddenly faced his friends who were laughing out loudly.

– You two fools, what have you done to me? – he asked testily.

Instead of replying to the question, the Breeze and the Zeppelin kept looking up at something well above the head of the Sunflower.

The Sunflower turned around himself, slowly raised his head and then suddenly he got it: The Sun!!! Oh, my God!!! The Sun did not hide behind the mountain as it was usual at this time of the day. To the contrary. The valley was basking in the warm sunlight and the Sunflower straightened himself up happily. As the dizziness receded the explanation dawned on him.

He was on the *other side* of the mountain!!! This was the other valley!!! This could only have been done by his friends, those two scoundrels. He turned back to them to say a heartfelt thank you but they were already gone, above the clouds.

When they returned in the evening, the Sunflower said:

– I am honestly very grateful for this wonderful surprise. You two are my best friends. The two craziest ones, too, - he added incredulously, but the best ones, and I really appreciate what you did.

– Can I have one more request?

The Breeze and the Zeppelin nodded simultaneously.

– Would you take me back to the other side? To my valley? You know, the Oak Tree...

– He must be bored without me...

XVII

Above the clouds

The Zeppelin and the Breeze soared to the sky holding their breath. They only burst into laughing when they reached the clouds. They were watching from here as the Sunflower and the Oak Tree fought about which side of the mountain is better.

When they relaxed, the Zeppelin asked – Who else it is that you want to ask? The Breeze answered without a second of hesitation.

The Zeppelin almost started to free fall in his astonishment. He could only make his enormous body upright again using his propellers that had 'Rock and roll never dies' sprayed all over them.

– You know him? – asked the Breeze surprisedly.

– I do not know him. But he knows me – replied the Zeppelin enigmatically. The Breeze contemplated this for a long time.

XIX

Japanese Garden – Dieue-sur-Meuse

– I missed you – greeted him the Woman – did you get answers to your questions?

– In many cases, yes – replied the Breeze – but there's still a lot of confusion in my head.

– What are you going to do?

– Have to ask one more person before I could decide.

– Who?

Then the Breeze told the Woman of his intention to ask the Man in a Hat who never said anything.

The Woman got suddenly very solemn. The expression in her black eyes was one the Breeze never saw before and seemingly her breathing got faster.

– Who is He, after all? – burst out the question from the Breeze.

– His name is Attila – replied the Woman – He is the entire Universe in just one person. He's the one, who's been looking at things for a hundred generations, things that we just noticed. The only one feared by the wicked. If, one day, he stands up, drops his overcoat and calls out to the world, then the sinners will pay for what they did. That will usher in a new era where conscience will grow and humans cease hurting each other at last.

– Can I ask him about a matter of such insignificance? – asked the Breeze with a hint of doubt in his voice.

– I don't know – replied Woman – nobody ever heard him talking, but might make an exception with you. Go ahead and good luck!!

XX

Quay – Ferencvaros

The Man in the Hat quietly watched the peel of the watermelon floating by on the waves of the river.

The Breeze was floating in the air opposite to him, hardly an inch above the waves and patiently waited for the answer to his question asked in a quivering voice.

After an amount of time that seemed close to eternity the Man in the Hat raised his head and looked at him. The Breeze never saw his eyes before. This look made him go numb, head-to-toe.

Good Lord, thought the Breeze to himself, Mankind's every virtue and failure, every sin and triumph are all there in his eyes, let alone every suffering! How can this Man take upon his shoulders all the suffering of Humans?

This piercing look made him weak. He, who can look that way, can never be lied to, doesn't ask for or give absolution, knows, understands and tolerates everything.

I could never make Him sleep, thought the Breeze.

The Man in the Hat then nodded briefly, silently and unmistakably. Then he pulled his hat down over his eyes again and returned to his thoughts.

XXI

Top of the world – Dents Du Midi

The Breeze was sitting on the protruding rock again. He didn't feel any tiredness although it was very late. To the contrary, he was energized by some force that he never experienced before, he suddenly felt himself indestructible, his entire being trembling with energy.

He slowly ran his gaze across the continent below, then all of a sudden he jumped, avalanched from the peaks of the Alps, ran over forests, fields, mountains and valleys, he crossed the Rhein, whizzed by the Acropolis and brought sleepness and dreams to the dwellers of cities and villages, relief to the suffering ones, absolution to all who were alone, in fear or in pain, who dreaded the tomorrow; relaxed the muscles of the miserable ones besieging the tunnel of Calais in search of a better life; to old folks left alone, laying helplessly on hospital beds who could only see him through the hospital windows as he was flying by; to children who didn't want to wake up again to live with their abusive parents; he just flew and flew and flew, skirting the top of the trees and wherever he went, people forgot to cry, wrinkles have smoothened, air got into thirsty lungs and once, just once, those who deserve shame had to cower, whimpering; he didn't fly the flags of fanaticism; instead he brought dreams and relief to human bodies twisted in hard work, to lovers left out in the cold, to orphaned eyes; he flapped his wings and peace took over the souls, while the Black Forest was rustling protectively,

and he didn't quit, until a peaceful slumber reigned over our home,

the good old Europe.